The Twelve Days of
HALLOWEEN

story by Leann Schwandt Lehner

illustrations by Alais Fortier-Meyer

Library of Congress Cataloging-in-Publication data available upon request.

ISBN (hardcover): 978-1-7374935-01
ISBN (ebook): 978-1-7374935-1-8

Cover design by Alais Fortier-Meyer.

Printed in the United States.

Oh Really Darling, LLC
Lake Mills, WI 53551

First Edition: August 2021

10 9 8 7 6 5 4 3 2 1

To all who love Halloween.
-L.S.L.

a vampire bat in a dead tree.

On the second day of Halloween,
my True Ghoul gave to me two scaredy-cats

and a vampire bat in a
dead tree.

On the third day of Halloween,
my True Ghoul gave to me three witch hats,

two scaredy-cats,
and a vampire bat in a dead tree.

On the fourth day of Halloween,
my True Ghoul gave to me
four broomsticks whirling,

three witch hats,

two scaredy-cats,

and a vampire bat in a dead tree.

On the fifth day of Halloween,
my True Ghoul gave to me
FIVE GOLD GOURDS!

four broomsticks whirling, three witch hats,
two scaredy-cats, and a vampire bat in a dead tree.

On the sixth day of Halloween,
my True Ghoul gave to me six spiders spinning,

FIVE GOLD GOURDS! four broomsticks whirling, three witch hats, two scaredy-cats, and a vampire bat in a dead tree.

six spiders spinning,
FIVE GOLD GOURDS!
four broomsticks whirling,
three witch hats,
two scaredy-cats,
and a vampire bat
in a dead tree.

On the eighth day
of Halloween,
my True Ghoul
gave to me
eight bones a-clacking,

seven pumpkins grinning, six spiders spinning,
FIVE GOLD GOURDS! four broomsticks whirling,
three witch hats, two scaredy-cats, and
a vampire bat in a dead tree.

On the ninth day of Halloween,
my True Ghoul gave to me nine ghosts boo-booing,

eight bones a-clacking, seven pumpkins grinning,
six spiders spinning, **FIVE GOLD GOURDS!**
four broomsticks whirling, three witch hats,
two scaredy-cats, and a vampire bat in a dead tree.

On the tenth day of Halloween,
my True Ghoul gave to me ten owls hoot-hooting,

nine ghosts boo-booing,
eight bones a-clacking,

seven pumpkins grinning, six spiders spinning,
FIVE GOLD GOURDS!
four broomsticks whirling, three witch hats,
two scaredy-cats, and a vampire bat in a dead tree.

On the eleventh day of Halloween,
my True Ghoul gave to me
eleven masks a-hiding,

Ten owls hoot-hooting,
nine ghosts boo-booing,
eight bones a-clacking,
seven pumpkins grinning,
six spiders spinning,
FIVE GOLD GOURDS!
four broomsticks whirling,
three witch hats, two scaredy-cats,
and a vampire bat in a dead tree.

On the twelfth day of Halloween,
my True Ghoul gave to me
twelve bats a-swooping,

Eleven masks a-hiding,
ten owls hoot-hooting,
nine ghosts boo-booing,
eight bones a-clacking,
seven pumpkins grinning,
six spiders spinning,

FIVE GOLD GOURDS!
four broomsticks whirling,
three witch hats,
two scaredy-cats,
and a vampire bat in a dead tree.

The End

CPSIA information can be obtained
at www.ICGtesting.com
Printed in the USA
BVRC100833240821
615123BV00008B/209